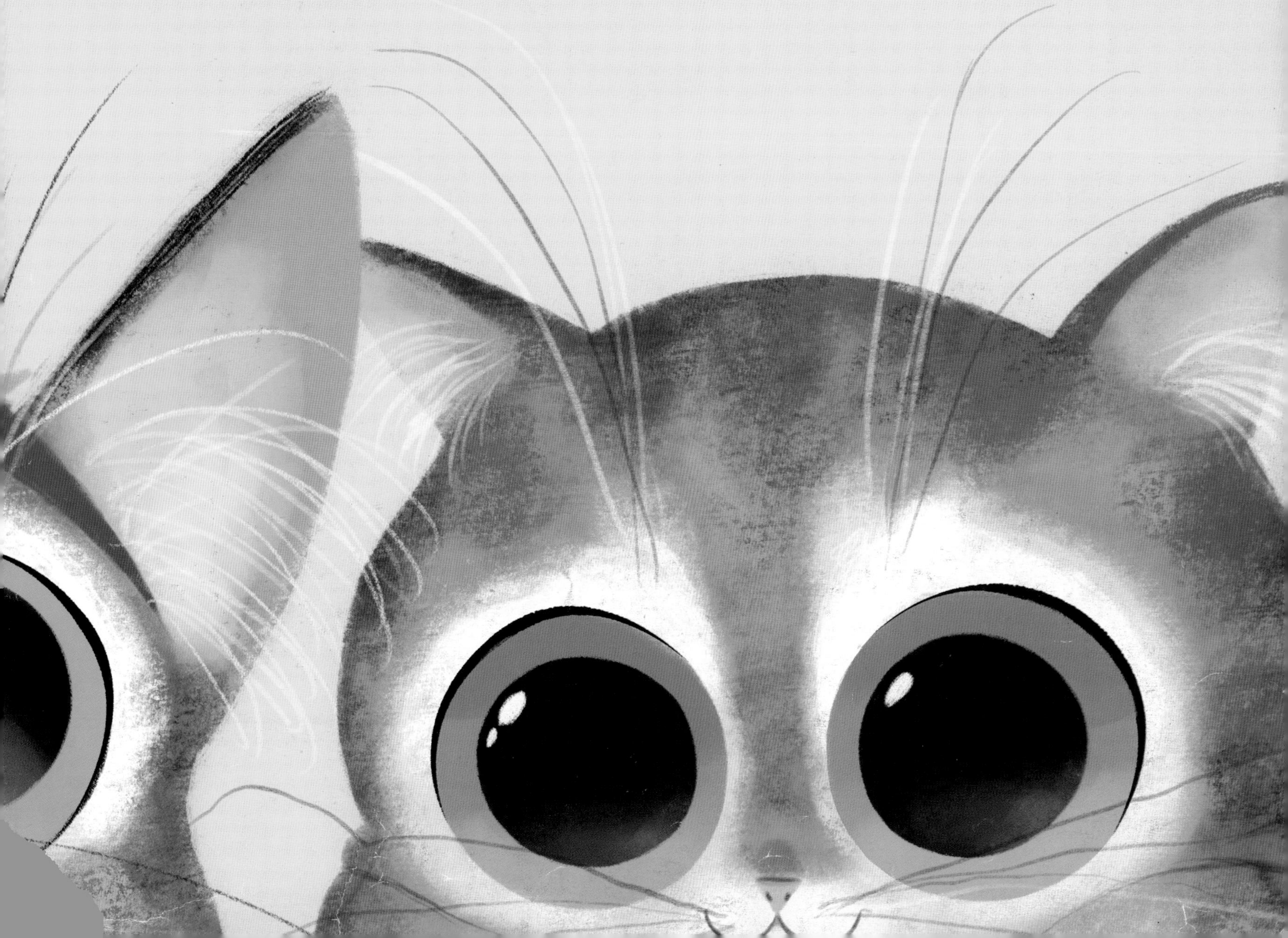

For Dee Dee, who makes everything better
—J.J.S.

For Mimi
—D.M.

Library of Congress Cataloging-in-Publication Data
Names: Shaffer, Jody Jensen, author. | Mottram, Dave, illustrator.
Title: Emergency Kittens! / written by Jody Jensen Shaffer ; illustrated by Dave Mottram.
Description: First edition. | New York : Doubleday Books for Young Readers, [2020] |
Summary: Introduces Emergency Kittens Mimi, Twee-Twee, and Adorbs, superheroes willing to help anyone in need.
Identifiers: LCCN 2019016292 (print) | LCCN 2019019021 (ebook)
ISBN 978-1-9848-3008-1 (hc) | ISBN 978-1-9848-3009-8 (glb) | ISBN 978-1-9848-3010-4 (ebk)
Subjects: | CYAC: Superheroes—Fiction. | Cats—Fiction. | Animals—Infancy—Fiction. | Humorous stories.
Classification: LCC PZ7.1.S4745 (ebook) | LCC PZ7.1.S4745 Eve 2020 (print) | DDC [E]—dc23

Book design by Nicole de las Heras

MANUFACTURED IN CHINA
10 9 8 7 6 5 4 3 2 1
First Edition

EMERGENCY KITTENS!

Jody Jensen Shaffer ★ Dave Mottram

Doubleday Books for Young Readers

Are you in a tough spot?

Has life got you down?

Maybe you need a superhero!
Someone muscly and fierce, possibly wearing tights.

Or maybe you need . . .

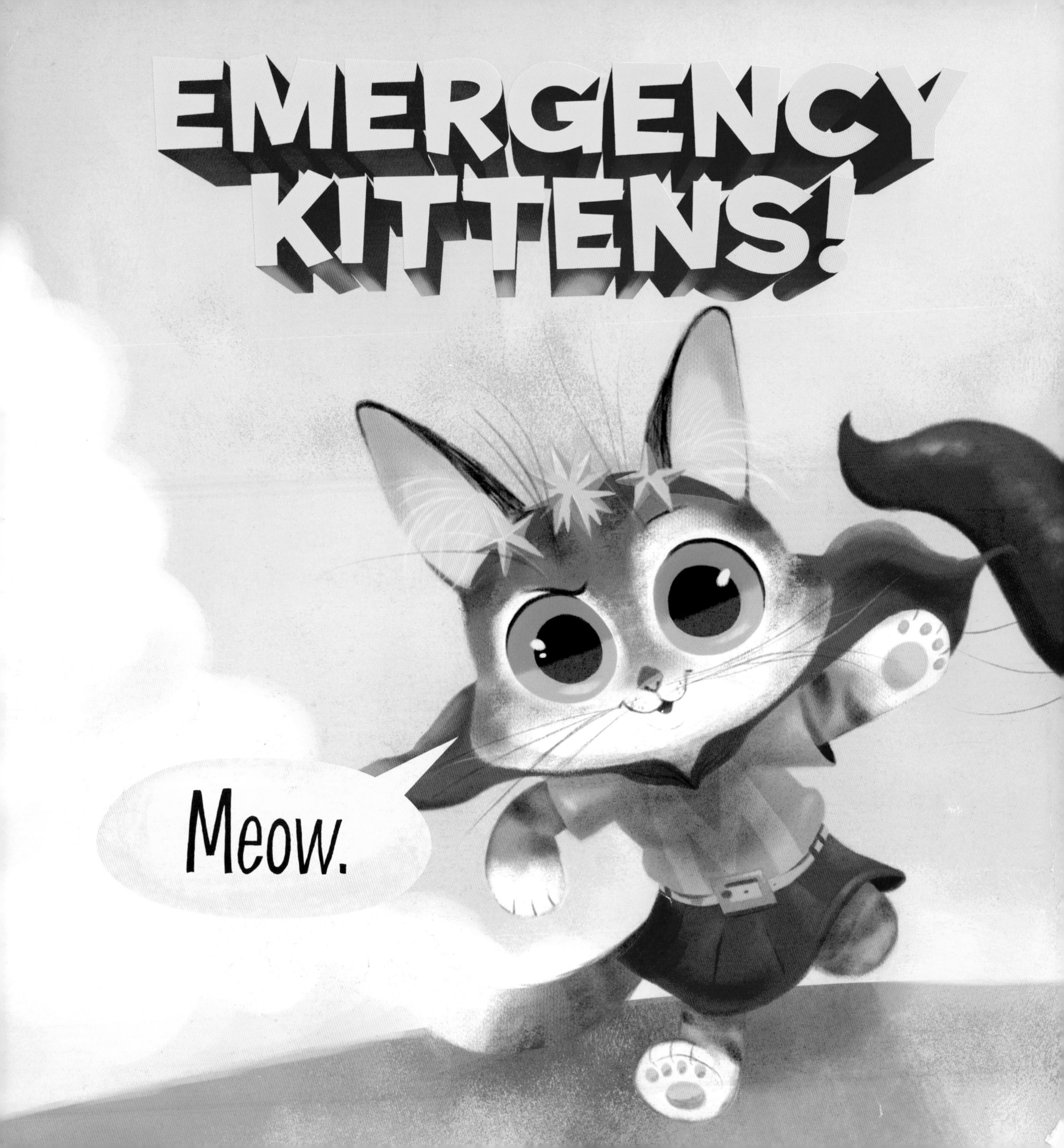
EMERGENCY KITTENS!
Meow.

Meet Mimi, Twee-Twee, and Adorbs!
These three cuties make everything better!

Meow.

Hi!

Jamie drops her ice cream cone.
Chin up, Jamie!

You've got EMERGENCY KITTENS!

Thanks,
EMERGENCY
KITTENS!

Oscar gets a bad haircut.

Or does he?

Emma gets stuck in a tree . . .
until EMERGENCY KITTENS save the day!

We're EMERGENCY KITTENS! We make everything better!

Unfortunately, not everyone knows about EMERGENCY KITTENS.
Meet Sheldon.

One day when Sheldon is playing, his ball takes a bad bounce.

My ball! Someone, help!

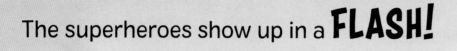

The superheroes show up in a **FLASH!**

#CRIMEFIGHTER

To the playground and beyond!

They lift bulldozers, leap buildings,
and tie themselves in knots.

HEY!

And finally . . .
finally . . .
after all that . . .

. . . they still can't get Sheldon's ball.

If superheroes can't help me, who can?

Well.
Mimi, Twee-Twee, and Adorbs
know the answer!

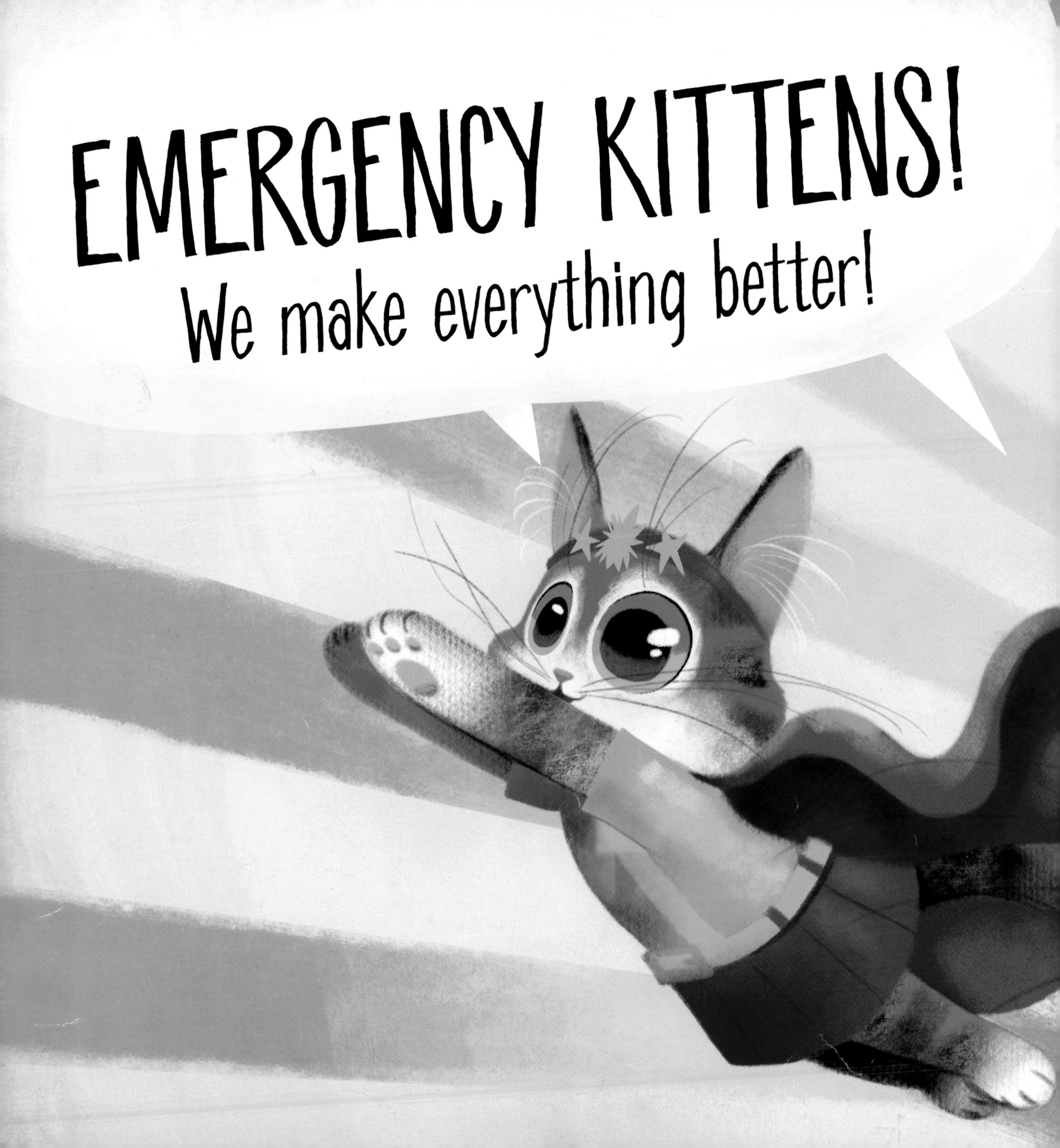
EMERGENCY KITTENS!
We make everything better!

The EMERGENCY KITTENS leap and spin,
bat and stretch, climb and tumble.

They knead and scratch,
chase and pounce. . . .

And then they get *really* serious. . . .

And honestly, who can resist that?

We're
EMERGENCY KITTENS!
We're always here
FUR you!